SpongeBob's Book of
Spooky Jokes

Stephen Hillenburg

Based on the TV series *SpongeBob SquarePants*® created by Stephen Hillenburg as seen on Nickelodeon®

SIMON SPOTLIGHT
An imprint of Simon & Schuster Children's Publishing Division
1230 Avenue of the Americas, New York, New York 10020

Manufactured in the United States of America
First Edition
8 10 9 7
ISBN-13: 978-1-4169-4735-6
ISBN-10: 1-4169-4735-3
0610 OFF

Scared Silly!

SpongeBob's Book of Spooky Jokes

by David Lewman

Simon Spotlight/Nickelodeon
New York London Toronto Sydney

Who's yellow, porous, and spooky?

SpongeBob ScarePants!

Boo!

Boo!

What happened to SpongeBob after Sandy told him a spooky story about cows?

He kept having night*moo*-ers.

Boo!

What's the difference between SpongeBob's pet and a ghostly claw?

One's a snail named Gary, and the other's a nail that's scary.

What does Sandy call a scary dream about acorns?

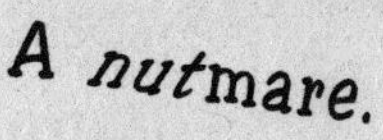

A *nut*mare.

What's the difference between a ghost's handshake and Mr. Krabs?

One's a creepy grab, and the other's a greedy crab.

What do monsters shout out at midnight on December 31?

"Happy New Fear!"

SpongeBob: Are sea fossils ever scared?

Squidward: They're more than scared—they're petrified!

Sandy: Did the ghosts like each other?
Pearl: Oh, yes, it was love at first fright.

SpongeBob: Where do you go to mail a letter to a ghoul?

Mrs. Puff: The ghost office.

Patrick: Which plant do ghosts like best?

Plankton: Bam*boo*!

Sandy: What do ghosts use to wash their hair?

SpongeBob: Sham*boo*!

Why is Mr. Krabs afraid of ghosts?

He's afraid they'll go through his wallet.

Why did Plankton hire a ghost chef?

It could always scare up something to eat.

Patrick: What do ghosts love to play at parties?

Pearl: Musical scares!

SpongeBob: Why did the fish act brave around the fisherman?

Plankton: He didn't want to look like a scaredy-catch.

Does the Flying Dutchman ever leave Bikini Bottom without scaring anyone?

No, he won't give up without a fright.

What did SpongeBob say when the ghoul wanted to haunt his house?

"Be my ghost!"

SpongeBob: When's the best time to look through a phantom?

Mermaid Man: When the ghost is clear.

Patrick: Why did the spirit haunt the TV station?

Sandy: He wanted to be a talk-show ghost.

Mr. Krabs: What colors are on the ghost flag?

Squidward: Red, white, and *boo*!

Patrick: What do you get when you cross a fish and a giant dinosaur?

Plankton: *Cod*zilla.

Patrick: What do ghosts sing to their babies?

SpongeBob: Lulla*boos*.

Squidward: What did the ghost say to the wall?

Sandy: "Just passing through."

What's the difference between a ghost and Plankton?

One's a floating ghoul, and the other's a gloating fool.

Mermaid Man: What do spiders eat at picnics?

Sandy: Corn on the cobweb.

Boo!

Boo!

Boo!

Boo!

SpongeBob: Which snake gives the prettiest presents?

Sandy: The bow constrictor.

Squidward: Where did the ghost learn about camping?

Sandy: From the Ghoul Scouts.

Patrick: What kind of TVs do ghosts have?

Squidward: Wide scream.

What's the difference between a ghost and Plankton?

One loves to make you scream, and the other loves to make new schemes.

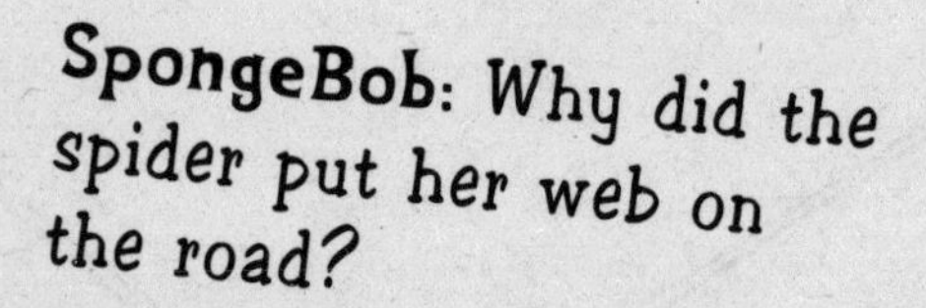

SpongeBob: Why did the spider put her web on the road?

Patrick: She wanted to go for a spin.

Mr. Krabs: What do monsters eat for breakfast?

SpongeBob: Peaches and scream.

Mrs. Puff: What did the dentist say to the vampire?

Squidward: "You look fangtastic!"

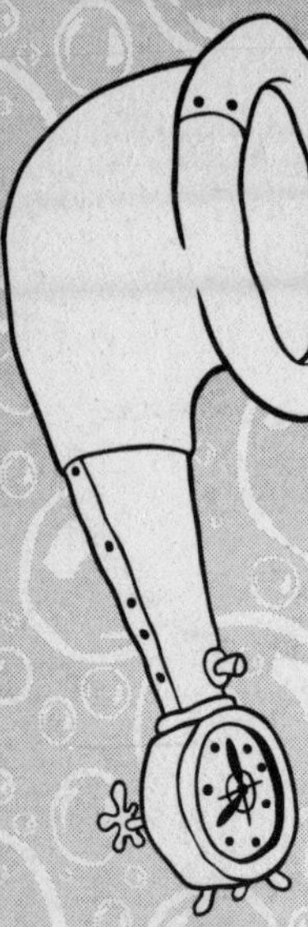

SpongeBob: Do clocks get scared?

Sandy: No, they get alarmed!

Squidward: What has long fangs, a big cape, and a round shell?

SpongeBob: A clam-pire!

Why did SpongeBob think Mrs. Puff was going to catch a chief vampire?

She said she was going to take a head count.

Sandy: When's the best time to catch vampire fish?

SpongeBob: When they're not biting.

Mr. Krabs: How did Dracula do in the vampire race?
Squidward: He won by a neck.
Boo!
Boo!
Boo!
When is Squidward like a vampire?
When he's a pain in the neck.

Patrick: What did the vampire say as he fell in the ocean?

Sandy: "I want to suck your . . . blub . . . blub . . . blub . . ."

What does SpongeBob turn into whenever the moon is full?

A squarewolf.

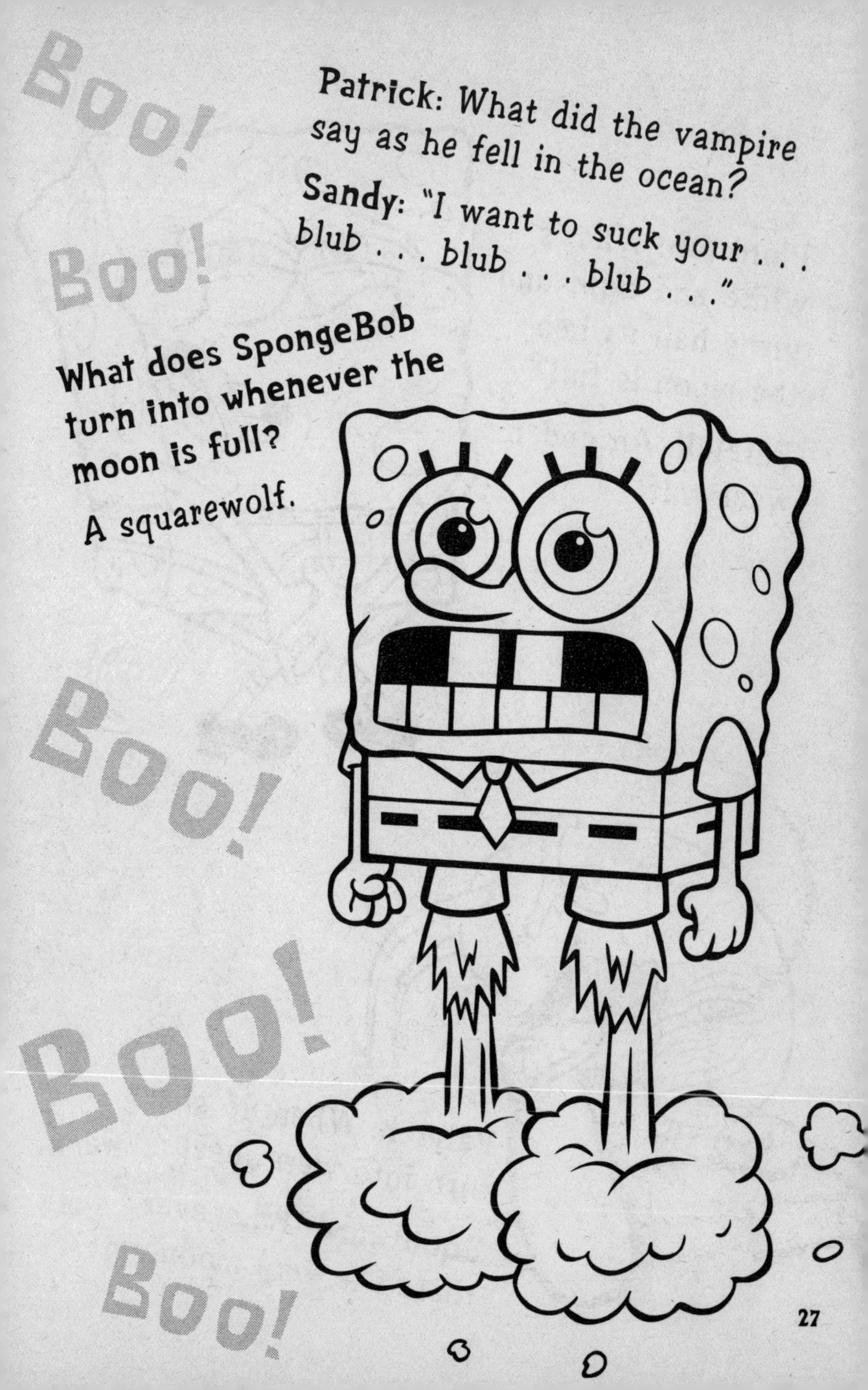

Plankton: What's white and tight and turns hairy when the moon is full?

Patrick: An underwearwolf.

Patrick: When do sheep turn into were-sheep?

Squidward: Whenever there's a wool moon.

SpongeBob: Why was the werewolf thrown out of the basketball game?

Pearl: For a technical howl.

Who haunts the Seven Seas and is great at jumping rope?

The Flying Double-Dutchman.

Mr. Krabs: Which monster is big and green and complains a lot?

Squidward: Frankenwhine.

SpongeBob: What's the difference between a fisherman and a witch?

Mrs. Puff: One casts hooks, and the other casts a hex.

Mr. Krabs: What do you get when you cross a witch and a dinosaur?

Squidward: Tyrannosaurus Hex.

Sandy: What's the difference between a purse and a witch who plays an instrument?

Mrs. Puff: One's a handbag, and the other's a band hag.

SpongeBob: Who always comes right after the aliens?

Patrick: The *b*-liens.

SpongeBob: Why are aliens so weird?

Patrick: Uh, maybe because they come from odder space.

Patrick: How do alien potatoes travel?

SpongeBob: In a space chip.

Sandy: Where do alien fish come from?

Mr. Krabs: Chowder space.

Sandy: Did the zombie enjoy the graveyard party?

SpongeBob: Yes, he had the tomb of his life.

Patrick: Why do zombies make good reporters?

Squidward: They always meet their deadlines.

SpongeBob: What's the difference between a funeral director and a pirate?

Mr. Krabs: One's an undertaker, and the other's a plunder taker.

Patrick: Why did the vampire fly into the bell?

Squidward: He wanted to be a dingbat.

SpongeBob: Are vampires loyal?

Mr. Krabs: Yes, they'll always go to bat for you.

BOO!

BOO!

SpongeBob: Why did the vampire fly to the baseball field?

Sandy: It was his turn at bat.

BOO!

Why did Patrick try to rescue the Egyptian queen from her tomb?

He'd heard Mr. Krabs say you should always save your mummy.

Patrick: Why are mummies wrapped in bandages?

Squidward: Oh, just be gauze, Patrick.

Boo!

Boo!

Boo!

Pearl: What happened to the young mummy who misbehaved?

Mrs. Puff: He got sent to his tomb.

SpongeBob: What kind of music do mummies like?

Squidward: Wrap.

Which spooky story is about a mad scientist who turns himself into a Krabby Patty?

"Dr. Jekyll and Mr. Fried."

Why did Patrick bring a mechanical man along in his boat?

He thought it was a row-bot.

Boo!

Boo!

Mrs. Puff: Why was the skeleton late to school?

Sandy: Her dog kept burying her!

Boo!

Boo!

What does Squidward have under his skin?

A scowl-eton.

Boo!

Boo!

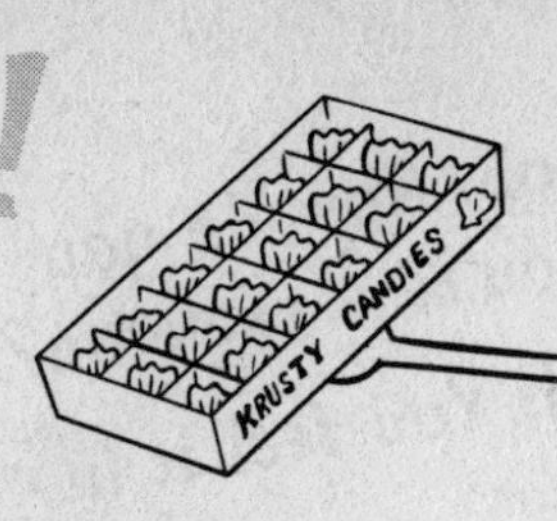

SpongeBob: What's a skeleton's favorite dessert?

Patrick: Chocolate bone-bones.

Boo!

Boo!

Sandy: Why couldn't the skeleton fall in love?

Mrs. Puff: He had a heart of bone.

Boo!

SpongeBob: How do you know if you're a skeleton?

Squidward: You feel it in your bones.

Why did the skeleton take so many towels to Goo Lagoon?

He wanted to stay bone-dry.

SpongeBob: What's covered in wool and full of aliens?

Sandy: A Ewe-F-O.

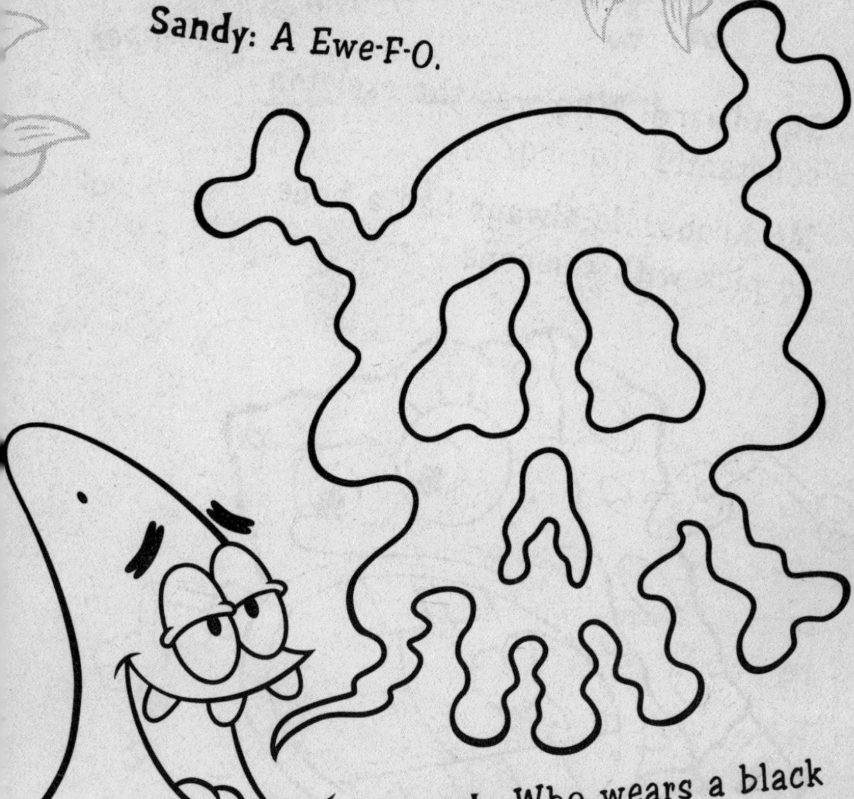

Patrick: Who wears a black robe and smells terrible?

Squidward: The Grim Reeker.

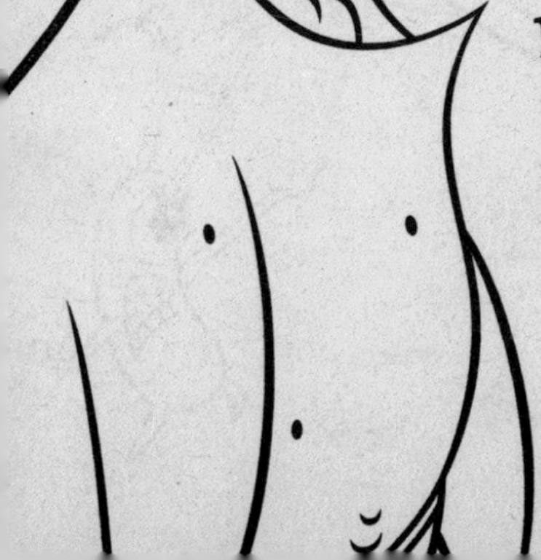

SpongeBob: Who wears a black robe and makes up great rhymes?

Sandy: The Grim Rapper.

Squidward: Why was the skeleton constantly arguing?

Mr. Krabs: He always had a bone to pick with someone.

Pearl: Which vampire feels at home in the water?
Plankton: Count Quackula.
What scary creature lives under Patrick's bed?
The Loch Mess Monster.

How did SpongeBob feel when a face appeared in his bowl of Kelpo?

A chill ran up his spoon.

Why does Patrick think darkness is heavy?

Because it isn't light.

Why did Patrick think Squidward's nose was scared?

It was running.

Mr. Krabs: When is a fisherman spooky?

SpongeBob: When he casts a shadow.

Scare
ya
later!